Rabbit in the Moon

Rabbit in the Moon

HAIKU

Raymond Roseliep

ALEMBIC PRESS
Plainfield, Indiana

Grateful acknowledgment is made to the editors of the following pub-
lications in which most of the poems in this book first appeared:
Abraxas, The Alchemist (Canada), *Alembic, August Derleth Society
Newsletter, Blue Buildings, The Blue Canary, Brussels Sprout, The
Christian Century, Cicada* (Canada), *Delta Epsilon Sigma Journal,
e.g.* (Saint Joseph's College, Maine), *Frogpond* (Haiku Society of
America), *Geppo Haiku Journal, Guts & Grace, HAI* (Japan), *High/
Coo, Inkstone* (Canada), *Kyōkason* (Japan), *The Lead Rush Review,
Mainichi Daily News* (Japan), *Midwest Poetry Review, Milkweed
Chronicle, Modern Haiku, Muse-Pie, The New Jersey Poetry Journal,
Outch* (Japan), *Outlet* (Loras College), *Pilgrimage, Poetry Now, Portals,
Quarry* (Canada), *The Spoon River Quarterly, Telegraph Herald* (Du-
buque), *Tightrope, Virtual Image, Wind Chimes, The Witness* (Dubuque),
and *Yankee.*

Typography by G.S. Lithographers,
 Carlstadt, New Jersey

Printed and bound by McNaughton & Gunn,
 Ann Arbor, Michigan

Library of Congress Cataloging in Publication Data

Roseliep, Raymond, 1917–
 Rabbit in the moon.

 1. Haiku, American.   I. Title.
PS3535.O675R3   811'.52   83-6445
ISBN 0-934184-15-1
ISBN 0-934184-16-X (soft)

1 2 3 4 5

Poems making their first appearance in anthologies include: "owl" (p. 73) and "bird landing" (p. 108), *Enter the Heart of the Fire: A Collection of Mystical Poems,* edited by Mary E. Giles and Kathryn Hohlwein (California State University, Sacramento, 1981); "After Solomon" (p. 64), *Erotic Haiku,* edited by Rod Willmot (Black Moss Press, Windsor, Ontario, 1983); and "child / in a window" (p. 19), *Knock at a Star: A Child's Introduction to Poetry,* edited by X.J. Kennedy and Dorothy M. Kennedy (Little, Brown and Company, Boston, 1982).

In the Foreword, the quotations from Cor van den Heuvel's *The Haiku Anthology* (Anchor Books, Anchor Press/Doubleday, Garden City, 1974, p. xxxii) are used with his permission.

"horizon" (p. 42) won the Harold G. Henderson Award, 1982, from the Haiku Society of America.

"observing the drought" (p. 47) received the California First Bank Award, 1982, from the Yuki Teikei Haiku Society of the United States of America and Canada.

"no wave today" (p. 86) merited First Place in the season word category, 1982, in the Hawaii Education Association's fifth annual contest.

"Birthday: II" (p. 55), originally titled "Birthday Poem for Peggy," was given Third Prize by *Yankee* magazine, 1981, in its annual roundup of Poetry Awards.

Sobi-Shi, who appears in a number of these poems, is the author's haigo or haiku name.

The title poem (p. 37) of this collection recalls one of the tales in the *Jātaka Book* dealing with the 550 states of existence, as animal or human, of the Buddha prior to his final birth as Gautama. In one of these earlier incarnations the Buddha is a rabbit in the moon.

Alembic Press is grateful to the National Endowment for the Arts, a Federal agency, for a grant which supported the publication of this book.

for Wanda Wallis

cloud
over the dove
mourning

above the keys
your fingers
shadow too

after music
the silence
of it

Foreword by the Author

WESTWORD WESTWARD

In the Introduction to his admirable *The Haiku Anthology,* editor Cor van den Heuvel writes: "The distinction between haiku and senryu, which are structurally similar, has . . . been a subject of controversy. Haiku is said to relate human nature to nature in general, while senryu is concerned primarily with human nature and is often humorous; but it is hard to draw the line." Then he notes that he has not tried to separate the senryu from the haiku in this anthology, though "there are a few that would be considered senryu even by their authors."

Like a good number of the classical Japanese writers who did not often make a clear distinction between the two forms, and like Mr. van den Heuvel editing the work of Western contemporaries, many of us writing in English do not attach definite labels to each of our poems in this Japanese-inspired genre. And so, as I did in my previous collections, for *Rabbit in the Moon* I am using *Haiku* for the book's sub-title, quite aware that I have senryu here as well as haiku that contain some of the spirit and one or more of the qualities of senryu.

With deliberation, too, I am including in my book several poems constructed of what I call haiku-stanzas. Some of these stanzas are haiku which can stand alone; some may send the reader back to the poem's title to complete or capture the haiku moment; or the stanzas advancing in their movements toward a unity may generate haiku enlightenment. These experiments are one more facet of my deep-rooted belief that the adventurers among us will continue hauling our Westword cargo Westward.

hole in my sock
letting spring
in

my father's back
loaded with me
and other frogs

hiking with him . .
a railroad track
the yellow brick road

arrow in the bird
the arrow of
my boy body

       sprout
       of marijuana:
       my first burr haircut

              father's oil lamp
              in the dawn
              my body's milk

two butterflies
love-knot
the air

maple seed
my wings
in you

with their pipes
hunched under spring sky
old men make clouds

lily
weighting the child
with it

in water
my body
of water

Big Dipper:
the frog's
soft drunken smile

child
in a window:
knock at the moon

footbridge
only the moon
crossing

butterfly
unshaking
on my nose shaking

for Charles M. Schulz
after his lepidopteran sequence

before the song
he draws the singer
in the egg

for Jon Vlakos

looking for the bird
who called
my name

HUMMINGBIRD

whisper
weight

eye-
wink

air

her peach bloom;
the soap smell
of a man

garden glove.
dried in the shape of
the touch on her breast

TRYST FOR LI HO

gauze of mist and gown
one disclosing
redbuds

flagleaves braided
gold cicada hairpin
fall

lute girl
heaven queen
in the fish bubble

clothesline
　　Sobi-Shi's pajamas
　　kicking the sun

the firefly
acting like he knows
Sobi-Shi's swan song

　　　　never alone
　　　　Sobi-Shi and the big dog
　　　　in the southern sky

gregorian chant
gracing
cocktail hour

nibbling
her martini olive:
"My best mood is rain"

bubbles
in the vial of rosebud
on her breast

two
descending a staircase:
the cat's suppler joints

for X. J. Kennedy

out of
the parlor window
Debussy's faun

armload of child
unloaded . . .
    the weight of night

midnight
in her spool cabinet
whirring

    feather bed
the short silence
before dawn

hanging from the eaves
little chimes
of my mother's earrings

aroma
of my shirt still warm
from her iron

her hourglass figure
in
my father's watch

downpour:
my "I-Thou"
T-shirt

.

new moon:
the finger
lost

.

your hair
bee gold
on the move

wildwood
where your hand
clings more

before love:
the meadowlark's
alarm note

first star
and our last gray
step

mist
on my mouth
air you touched

field daisies
in the kitchen
        our strangeness

        sun behind
the pear-blossom bud:
its pink heart

petals fill
the space
you filled

child's tea:
we sip
clover

doll shop
a backward look at
the dried apple face

among violets
no one notices
the bishop's amethyst

matins:
rain smell
in the psalms

Merton's grave
bodhi tree
scratching moon

hugging the river's moon
ah, Li Po
I tried it too

log lifted,
light catches
the wood louse

zither soundbox
full of the lost soul
of a cricket

bird bone dust
earth receiving
itself

under rained-on
Buddha
the frog keeping dry

rabbit in the moon
in our broccoli
small buddha voices

rose
body language
of the bee

horizon
wild swan drifting through
the woman's body

willow wind
through your hair,
our boat drying

leave the dream
in the sand
where we slept

FIREFLY

that dark
miss
night

the within
and without
of us

we are not
our own
light

children dance
through stars or fireflies
—who'll say?

for Takahashi

Pike's Peak:
my mother's
"touch nothing"

afterglow
in folds of hill
and my father's neck

observing the drought
grandfather and a young bird—
one with cataracts

scarecrow:
the lapel
crucifix

tornado watch:
above our breathing
the cat's purr

birthday rain—
the old man's face
of the turtle

melons hoed,
old men sit
with their beer

Sobi-Shi cools
the stolen melon
in the baptismal font

lattice:
the green sight of him,
his brown touch

dark too
holds earth tones
of his field clothes

plucking geese;
the peacock's
"Eee-ooo-ii"

heat wave
stalling tiny traffic
on that grassblade

buttoning his fly
the boy with honeysuckle
clenched in his mouth

bird in hand
the stirrings
in a boy

the fly rocks
in the spider's hammock
wide awake

pear thief leaving
the moon gives back
his shadow

lost his mother.
the child looks
under a rock

BIRTHDAY: I

each night
a moon pares
peel by peel

whistling sky
down
to your heels

a second
being
your second being

BIRTHDAY: II

in water lilies
how old the face
of a cloud

milkweed
light flies
spun

you enter
your shadow
reborn

can't tell
the petal
from the kiss

love made,
twig
fire

vasectomy;
the doll's
eye

awed
by Auden
and fly song

in amber
bubble of air and wings
forever in flight

sculpturing
her lover
coming forever

her lover's whistle
in the evergreen
above his grave

green things
greener a love
ago

moon dog
among
the gone

reading Shakespeare
to the birds
      all lungs full

the unknown bird
with the rusty rump
sings anyway

THE EIGHTEENTH OF SEPTEMBER

(Katherine Anne Porter: 1890–1980)

on one so still
the shadow
of a bird

      out of what mist
      one hand still
      holding

            her one
            "we'll meet"
            still

THE MORNING–GLORY

waking
space

handles
light

circling
loss

for William R. Wilkins
KAP's secretary

AFTER SOLOMON

i

wild strawberries
        I taste
        my way

ii

hills fold around
        river
lover and lover

iii

Christ in hand
        swing gentle sac
        between my legs

the bee stops singing.
we find
who we are

autumn frog
what it is
the smile hides

in the bandshell
just autumn wind
and a few crickets

in Carnegie Hall
the janitor listens for
the sparrow

WILD GEESE

sky
of
themselves

hearing
only
themselves

beyond
our
selves

NOBEL RECIPIENT

in her sweater
crumbs the birds missed
in Calcutta

sitting with a lizard
soaking up
the silence of rock

swan curving into
its body curving
into the lake

owl:
our
whoness

C

          h
         g
        i
       h
Pavarotti's
bittersweet unsplit

autumn
my bronzed
baby shoes

wind drives the leaves,
the old follow
their canes

good *eye* closed,
Sobi-Shi views
the last leaves

my mother's picture—
bluejay with its autumn
"tull-ull"

searching
for my father
in the hunter's moon

CITYSCAPE

sky of no song,
the spaces
between people

brazier of chestnuts:
the vendor's
arthritic dance

from the fire
nothing salvaged
but the fire

in his shoes tonight
I go out to watch
the sky he swore by

the lull
between each apple
fall

you in apples,
Sobi-Shi picking one
on his lute

autumn crow
voicing   the void
in us all

earthshadow
on the moon:
mine on you

artist
doing the *eyes*
my kiss had closed

goose
flight,
mine

a leaf
breaks
the heart pump

intensive care:
high wire walking
souls

recovery room
clouds change
their names

recovery room
snow goose bound
for home

pacemaker
in your chest
the autumn cricket

my father's
birthplace
milkweed

no towel-snapping
brother
body of my brother

the light
in the eye
of the pine

your death
in the bird loud air
    no further word

willow
and your scarf
    unthreading

in the woods alone
the whiteness of my body
    though the moon comes

light springs
a wren note
and a half

bird still
the music
you've made

cicada dusk
Aunt Rachel's
keywound clock

she stops
crumbling bay leaf
for the Strauss oboe

no wave today
from my friend in the caboose
autumn wind

with mourners
the rabbit
a statue

balloon holding
the breath
of the gone

on stone he scratches
in pig Latin
his dead friend's name

after wood silence
your voice is far
from plain

your eyes' smoke:
Rembrandt's need
to paint light

you
and the earth
I roll with

SWINBURNE SHELF

the swing and sway
of the spider spinning

the "Ugh"
of Picasso's woman
ironing

children bobbing
through the pelvis
of Georgia O'Keeffe

steeplejacks:
souls too small
to have names

her *eyes*
on the skylark's route—
backpack of child

chilly *evening*:
the Mass priest borrows
a stranger's prayer shawl

Paul gone and I go
to light a candle
lit

monarch winded,
milkweed
in my beard

from my hand . . .
winghold
on the void

snow:
all's
new

sparrow pecking
an icicle,
I blow my coffee

waiting
for an old father
snow drifts

snow quits
in the moonless wood
is there

snowbound:
the music
in a man

your eyes
and winter sky
stars wear through

song and its bird frozen—
from my pocket
the key still warm

Pegasus
pawing the air—
    how still you are

winter night
your train goes
note by note

day comes
in little
pieces

air of snow
in David's town
    the passing whisperer

barn window:
a child calls
the dog star

chimes
no
wind

hay
where mice sleep
what whoop

hand
handing a child
for handling

ice floe
green soul
aboard

flakefall
helping the bell
ring a little

night window
click of pine
    my mother's needle

unlocking her room
this anniversary—
    wintergreen

        fog
    stairs find
    sky

"MORE LIGHT!"

—Goethe

land and light play:
glasses
grandparents share

*

phoenix pin
in her hair
we walk the moon home

*

wintergrove
the cry
of light

*

I am
what light
is here

*

cataract:
Lord, make
clay
(John 9:6)

gym shower:
the rose shape
of his war wound

bird landing
sky color
on its face

sky
of tree
and I

in sunlight too
her face is a tired
Renoir

egg:
sound of sand
sifting

109

with salt and lemon
Sobi-Shi rubs his brass chime,
leaving the wind spots

gone through a moon
Sobi-Shi still
on "Hold"

frost
on the bellrope
    the monk's snaggletooth

      kiss
   on a priesthand
    winter moth

                                       sleet
                                       hones
                                       farewell

slipping into
the back of my eyes,
her Noh mask off

eyes close
to keep sunset
          longer

WINTERSET

i

pressed in concrete
her hand and mine
iced

ii

over her bed
this old lover . .
a nerve kicks in

before his hearth:
trying on
her shadow

on my bed
her gloves
hold each other

my father's
"love enough and well"
deep winter

diabetic
nibbling pie;
      the winter bee

the clown's wife
at her needlepoint
clown

grandma's
cloudy eye—
      the last pinfeather

icicle
still
the knifegrinder's bell

in the sky
over my bed
his yellow tooth

my iceskates sharpened,
the geese walk
barefoot

sitting out
"The Beautiful Blue Danube"
with my drying socks

who lived here before
left a web
for the moon

so small a child
pushing clouds
from the moon

stranger in town
the otherness
of the moon

what is
in light
is light:

I am
all around
me

About the Author

Father Raymond Roseliep, a Ph.D. in English, was a faculty member at Loras College in Dubuque, Iowa, for twenty years, and was named Professor Emeritus in 1982. Since his retirement from teaching in 1966 he has been resident chaplain at Holy Family Hall, an infirmary of Franciscan nuns in Dubuque.

Widely published and recognized as a master of traditional English verse forms, Roseliep began experimenting with haiku in 1960; this is his eleventh collection of haiku to appear since 1976. Besides the major haiku periodicals which publish his work regularly, more than ninety other magazines in their various issues have printed his haiku, and he appears in many anthologies and in a growing number of textbooks. His haiku have attracted critical praise from such poets as the late W.H. Auden, Josephine Jacobsen, Denise Levertov, William Stafford, X.J. Kennedy, and A.R. Ammons.

Roseliep has won both of the two annual haiku contests held in North America, the Harold G. Henderson Award from the Haiku Society of America in 1977—and again in 1982, and the Shugyo Takaha Award (grand prize) from the Yuki Teikei Haiku Society of the United States and Canada in 1980. *Sailing Bones* won him first place in the Biennial Merit Book Awards from the Haiku Society of America in 1981. Listed among the Acknowledgments (p. 5) are his other recent awards for haiku which are presented in this book.

Other Books by the Author

The Linen Bands (The Newman Press, 1961)

The Small Rain (The Newman Press, 1963)

Love Makes the Air Light (W.W. Norton & Company, Inc., 1965)

Voyages to the Inland Sea, IV. Essays and Poems. Edited by John Judson. (University of Wisconsin—LaCrosse, 1974)

Flute Over Walden (Vagrom Chap Books, 1976)

Walk In Love (Juniper Press, 1976)

Light Footsteps (Juniper Press, 1976)

A Beautiful Woman Moves with Grace (The Rook Press, 1976)

Sun in His Belly (High/Coo Press, 1977)

Step on the Rain (The Rook Press, 1977)

Wake to the Bell (The Rook Press, 1977)

A Day in the Life of Sobi-Shi (The Rook Press, 1978)

Sailing Bones (The Rook Press, 1978)

Sky in My Legs (Juniper Press, 1979)

Firefly in My Eyecup (High/Coo Press, 1979)

The Still Point (Uzzano Press, 1979)

A Roseliep Retrospective: Poems & Other Words By & About Raymond Roseliep. Edited by David Dayton. (Alembic Press, 1980)

Listen to Light (Alembic Press, 1980)

Swish of Cow Tail (Swamp Press, 1982)